Publisher's note

Ancient Chinese classic poems are exquisite works of art. As far as 2,000 years ago, Chinese poets composed the beautiful work *Book of Poetry* and *Elegies of the South*. Later, they created more splendid Tang poetry and Song lyrics. Such classic works as *Thus Spoke the Master* and *Laws Divine and Human* were extremely significant in building and shaping the culture of the Chinese nation. These works are both a cultural bond linking the thoughts and affections of Chinese people and an important bridge for Chinese culture and the world.

Mr. Xu Yuanchong has been engaged in translation for 70 years. He won the Lifetime Achievement Award in Translation conferred by the Translators Association of China (TAC) in 2010, and won the "Aurora Borealis" Prize for Outstanding Translation of Fiction Literature, conferred by the Federation of International Translators (FIT) in 2014. He is honored as the only expert who translates Chinese poems into both English and French. After his excellent interpretation, many Chinese classic poems have been further refined into perfect English and French rhymes. This collection of Classical Chinese Poetry and Prose gathers his most representative English translations. It includes the classic works *Thus Spoke the Master, Laws Divine and Human* and dramas such as *Romance of the Western Bower, Dream in Peony Pavilion, Love in Long-life Hall* and *Peach Blooms Painted with Blood*. The largest part of the collection includes the translation of selected poems from different dynasties. The selection includes various types of poetry. The selected works start from the pre-Qin era to the Qing Dynasty, covering almost the entire history of classic poems in China. Reading these works is like tasting "living water from the source" of Chinese culture.

We hope this collection will help English readers "understand, enjoy and delight in" Chinese classic poems, share the intelligence of Confucius and Lao Tzu (the Older Master), share the gracefulness of Tang poems, Song lyrics and classic operas and songs and promote exchanges between Eastern and Western culture. We also sincerely invite precious suggestions from our readers.

出版前言

　　中国古代经典诗文是中国传统文化的奇葩。早在两千多年以前，中国诗人就写出了美丽的《诗经》和《楚辞》；以后，他们又创造了更加灿烂的唐诗和宋词。《论语》《老子》这样的经典著作，则在塑造、构成中华民族文化精神方面具有极其重要的意义。这些作品既是联接所有中国人思想、情感的文化纽带，也是中国文化走向世界的重要桥梁。

　　许渊冲先生从事翻译工作70年，2010年荣获"中国翻译文化终身成就奖"，2014年荣获国际译联颁发的"北极光"杰出文学翻译奖。他被称为将中国诗词译成英法韵文的唯一专家，经他的妙手，许多中国经典诗文被译成出色的英文和法文韵语。这套"许译中国经典诗文集"荟萃许先生最具代表性的英文译作，既包括《论语》《老子》这样的经典著作，又包括《西厢记》《牡丹亭》《长生殿》《桃花扇》等戏曲剧本，数量最多的则是历代诗歌选集。这些诗歌选集包括诗、词、散曲等多种体裁，所选作品上起先秦，下至清代，几乎涵盖了中国古典诗歌的整个历史。阅读和了解这些作品，即可尽览中国文化的"源头活水"。

　　我们希望这套许氏译本能使英语读者对中国经典诗文也"知之，好之，乐之"，能够分享孔子、老子的智慧，分享唐诗、宋词、中国古典戏曲的优美，并以此促进东西文化的交流。也敬请读者朋友提出宝贵意见。

PROJECT FOR TRANSLATION AND PUBLICATION
OF CHINESE CULTURAL WORKS

中国文化著作翻译出版工程项目

CLASSICAL CHINESE POETRY AND PROSE

SELECTED LYRICS OF TANG AND FIVE DYNASTIES

TRANSLATED BY XU YUANCHONG

许译中国经典诗文集

唐五代词选 | 许渊冲 译

五洲传播出版社
China Intercontinental Press

中华书局
Zhonghua Book Company

CONTENTS
目　　　录

CLASSICAL CHINESE POETRY AND PROSE

SELECTED LYRICS OF
TANG AND FIVE DYNASTIES

TRANSLATED BY XU YUANCHONG

China Intercontinental Press   Zhonghua Book Company

PREFACE

The word "lyric" used in this anthology refers to a poem composed to a certain tune. During the Tang Dynasty (618–907), the subject matter of a lyric often corresponded to the meaning of its tune title. For example, the *Magpie on the Branch*, a popular song selected here, deals with a magpie in the cage; the *Dream of a Maid of Honour*, the first literary lyric attributed to Li Bai, depicts the solitude of a young woman waking from the dream of her husband; Zhang Zhihe's A *Fisherman's Song* describes the happiness of a fisherman; Bai Juyi's *Everlasting Longing* depicts the longing of a young wife for the return of her husband; Liu Yuxi's *Ripples Sifting Sand* deals with the women washing gold from sand; Huangfu Song's *The South Recalled* reveals the poet's nostalgia for the Southern Country. Since the Late Tang, the subject of the lyric had gradually lost its thematic connection with the tune pattern.

In 1900, in a Buddhist monastery of Dunhuang were found the hand-copied manuscripts of over a thousand lyrics and songs which had been sealed and preserved there for almost a thousand years. Among the manuscripts we find a considerable number of popular songs that may be dated back to the Early Tang (c. 650) and that were sung during the Tang and Five Dynasties (907–960) period. Originally the lyric was considered a popular song form. The differences between a literary lyric and a popular song are as follows: (1) The former is characterized almost exclusively by the lyrical mode while the latter contains a variety of modes-narrative, dramatic and lyrical. For example, in the first popular song selected in this anthology, a dialogue is used to heighten the effect of dramatic action. (2) A popular song states feelings in a straightforward manner, simple and direct, while a literary lyric is subtle and refined. (3) The diction of the former is generally closer to the spoken, colloquial usage while that of the latter is literary.

Popular songs were composed by unknown poets or common people and sung by courtesans and musicians. The first literate who began to write lyrics was supposed to be Li Bai (701–762), whose two poems collected here deal with the sorrow of farewell and separation. Some scholars claimed that the *Buddhist Dancers* attributed to him was forgery for, in their view, that tune could not have been produced as early as the High Tang (c. 713–755). In fact, it was proved that in 742 a certain monk of Longxing Temple composed a song to the tune of *Buddhist Dancers*, which was found in the Thousand Buddha Caves at Dunhuang and is now preserved in the British Museum.

At first, the literary lyric was based on the poetics of the seven-charactered quatrain, which could be set to music during the High Tang. The favorite tunes among the literati poets of the Middle Tang were those whose song words were written in exactly the same pattern as the seven-charactered quatrain, for example, Bai Juyi's and Liu Yuxi's *Bamboo Branch Song* and *Willow Branch Song*. Gradually some popular tunes changed into different metrical patterns, for instance, Liu Yuxi's and Li Yu's *Ripples Sifting Sand*. The contribution of literati poets to the lyric is that, while the persona in popular songs often starts by expressing a particular feeling explicitly and then dwells on it throughout the poem, the literati poets combine carefully the persona's inner feeling and natural scenes to form a world of correspondence.

Wen Tingyun (812–870) was the most important literati poet of Late Tang, in whose hands lyric was transformed from mere song of entertainment to verse of high literary quality. One of the distinctive features of his style is the juxtaposition of scenes vaguely linked by the rhetoric of implicit meaning, which creates a sense of ambiguity admired by critics. "He often takes several harmonious colourful images" centered on the lives of women, says Yu Pingbo, "and randomly places them together, letting them blend naturally." "While the images of women are generally static and pictorial," says Kang-i Sun, "physical objects are often animated. This technique of inversion of animated and inanimated attributes has contributed greatly to the power of Wen's implicit rhetoric." But in his one-stanza lyric, for example, *Dreaming of the Southern Shore* selected here, we discover a style that is characterized by explicit expressions echoing the popular song

The popular songs exercised a greater influence on Wei Zhuang (836–910), whose poetic style is straightforward, direct, narrative and colloquial Wei did not have the peaceful life Wen had, so many of his poems express his nostalgia for the past and his sorrow over the dismal situation after the down-fall of the Tang Dynasty. This implies his painful realization of the discrepancy between a desirable wish and an undesirable reality and his disappointment in life. His lyrics include direct expression of personal feelings and autobiographical details as opposed to Wen's indirect depiction of feminine feelings. What he adds to the lyric reveals a reaction against the ornate style of Wen, who excels in writing poems with implicit meaning while Wei is famed for explicit poetry.

Li Yu (937–978), the last monarch of the Southern Tang (937–975), represents the highest achievement of the lyric poets during the Five Dynasties period. "Not until Li Yu," says Wang Guowei, "did lyric poets expand their field of vision and deepen their feelings. Consequently, the lyric of musical performers was transformed into that of literary scholars." Most of Li Yu's works are direct lyrical expression, revealing the depth of his private feelings. His unusual accomplishment was closely related to his personal experiences. Very few poets have gone through such a drastic change in the circumstance of their personal lives as he did. In his early years, as reigning emperor, he indulged in a luxurious life at court. After losing his kingdom to the Northern Song emperor in 976 and becoming a political prisoner in the Song capital, he began to live a life of suffering until his death four years later. The striking contrast of past and present provided him with the need to express his innermost feelings in poetry intensely lyrical.

In terms of rhetorical devices, he has followed the style of Wei who enhances the effect of subjective rhetoric, rather than that of Wen who creates deliberately an impersonal voice. Yet his lyric often seems far more subjective in tone than Wei's. One of his great achievements lies in his ability to use the simplest kind of sentence to express the most profound and complex emotions. Another is his creation of poetic images. To the poet, human emotions do not remain static; they grow and flow. Thus, the images of growing grass and flowing river are used to emphasize the temporal dimension and the changing nature of human feelings.

In point of characterization, we may say that Wen's poem is descriptive and static. The well-known image he used to describe the mental state of a deserted woman is a pair of birds, which subtly implies the loneliness of the persona. On the other hand, Wei's lyric is narrative and active, yet it is confined to the traditional stereotyped image of a woman in the chamber. By contrast, Li's images of women are quite unconventional. His success lies in his technique of focussing on certain unique movement performed by the character. In short, we may conclude that Wen's lyric is written with coloured ink, Wei's with bitter tears and Li's with the blood pouring out of his own heart.

Li Yu represents the highest achievement of the lyric poets in composing shorter poems.

Xu Yuanchong
Peking University
Dec. 1985

Lyrics from Dunhuang

TUNE: PHOENIX'S RETURN INTO THE CLOUD
COMPLAINT OF A WARRIOR'S WIFE

My warrior gone for years
Like duckweed in a foreign land.
Since then nor man nor word appears.
Is he lost in frost, or starlight?
I heard the washerwomen's pounding spread
And saw wild geese in southern flight
Lonely I slept in curtained bed.
In vain I dreamed of my husband
From night to night.

I complain of your unfeeling heart.
Why don't you think it better
For someone to write a letter
To express longings for my part?
I lean against the window, mute, with tears in my eyes.
What could I do but pray to sun and moon to rise?
What could I do but utter sighs?
The incense burned up as of yore,
What can I do but add some more?

TUNE: JOY OF PLAYING BALL
COMPLAINT AGAINST A YOUNG GALLANT

My silken dress is wet with tears.

How could I trust young gallant peers?

Should I neglect my sister's good advice:

"Do not give him your heart at all!"

I think it over twice or thrice:

Why should I answer his unfaithful call?

TUNE: BUDDHIST DANCERS
A THOUSAND VOWS

On the pillow we make a thousand vows, we say
Our love will last unless green mountains rot away,
On the water can float a lump of lead,
The Yellow River dries up to the bed.

Stars can be seen in broad daylight,
The Dipper in the south shines bright.
Even so, our love will not be done
Unless at midnight rises the sun.

TUNE: BUDDHIST DANCERS
SONG ON THE FRONTIER

In days of old good generals shone like star on star,

And moved barbarian tribes to submit from afar,

They put out on frontier war flame,

And won in royal tower their fame.

Now separated by the foe,

Oh, how can we express our woe!

When we've recovered the lost town,

We'll pay our homage to the crown.

TUNE: SILK-WASHING STREAM
A BOATMAN'S SONG

After passing the five-mile beach, the breeze stops blowing.

With sails put up, the boat seems light when we are rowing.

We use no scull and take our oars from water flowing,

But still the boat is going.

How sparkling waves rising with the wind catch the eye!

As if to welcome us, the mountain seems to come nigh.

On a close look, it does not move but towers high,

The boat is going by.

Note

This is a popular song unearthed at Dunhuang. It depicts the life and joy of a boatman.

TUNE: GAZING ON THE SOUTHERN SHORE
A RIVERSIDE WILLOW TREE

Don't pluck a sprig from me!
Or I tell you: too partial you will be.
I am a riverside willow tree.
My sprigs are plucked by the throng.
My love cannot last long.

TUNE: GAZING ON THE SOUTHERN SHORE
SONG OF A DESERTED WOMAN

The bright moon in the sky,
Viewed from afar, looks like silver on high.
When night grows deep, the pressing wind roars by.
Oh, wind, dispel the cloud veiling the moon, if you can,
To brighten the heart of my unfaithful man!

TUNE: CALMING THE WAVES
WORD AND SWORD

What is the use of word when you have sword to wield?

A bookworm can't compare with warriors in the field.

Green-tasseled spear in hand, against the foe you fight;

With a sword bright

As Dragon's fountain or the moon you kill their knight.

How we admire the warriors of olden days!

Don't boast that scholars are better in many ways!

What if you hear on four frontiers the war flame rise?

Ask scholars wise

Who's brave to calm the wind and waves under the skies?

TUNE: MAGPIE ON THE BRANCH
A PINING WOMAN AND A CAGED BIRD

How can I bear to hear the chattering magpie
Announcing happy news on which I can't rely?
So I catch it alive when it flies here again,
Shut it in a cage and let it lonely remain.

With good intent I brought her a happy message,
Who'd expect she'd shut me up in a golden cage!
I wish her husband would come back soon so that I
Might be set free and take my flight into the blue sky.

Note

This is a popular song written by an unknown poet of the Tang Dynasty (618–907) and unearthed in one of the chapels in the Thousand Buddha Caves at Dunhuang, Gansu, in 1900. Unlike a literary lyric in which everything is seen through the eye of the persona, this song presents two distinct points of view by using a dialogue between a woman who waiting in vein for the return of her husband, and a magpie who is supposed to announce the expected arrival.

TUNE: A SOUTHERN SONG
THE WIFE'S REPLY TO HER HUSBAND

Oh, since you went away,

Could my mind go astray?

Tears shed in dream left trace

On my scratched face.

I made a heart-shaped knot;

My ape-torn apron might not be forgot.

My hair is ruffled by the rosy screen,

My pin of gold

Is split as of old.

Lovesick of you, tear trace can still be seen.

Like pine or cypress trees.

Could I have pined for others, please?

Li Bai

Tune: Buddhist Dancers

O'er far-flung wooded plain wreaths of smoke weave a screen,
Cold mountains stretch into a belt of sorrowful green.
The dusk invades the tower high
Where someone sighs a longing sigh.

On marble steps she waits in vain
But to see birds fly back amain.
Where should she gaze to find her dear?
She sees but stations far and near.

Note

As early as the Northern Song Dynasty (960–1127), this poem and the following were considered to be the two earliest literary lyrics written by Li Bai (701–762). This poem describes the sorrow of a young woman who mounts a high tower at dusk, looks far into the wooded plain and the belt-like mountains, but fails to find her husband on his way home.

TUNE: DREAM OF A MAID OF HONOUR

The flute plays a sobbing tune,

She wakes from dreams when o'er her bower wanes the moon.

When o'er her bower wanes the moon,

Year after year green willows grieve

As from the Bridge the people leave.

All's merry on Clear Autumn Day,

But she receives no word from ancient northwest way.

And now o'er ancient northwest way

The sun declines, the west wind falls

O'er royal tombs and palace walls.

Note

This lyric depicts the solitude of a young woman who wakes from a dream of her husband on the eve of Clear Autumn Day or Mountain-climbing Day, that is, the 9th day of the 9th lunar month. It recalls his parting with her at the Bridge east of the capital. She then goes to the Merry-making Plain where she waits until sunset without seeing a messenger coming from her husband. Another commentator says that the people taking leave were those who were going to the war against the rebels in 755, so this lyric predicted the decline and fall of the Tang Empire.

Dai Shulun

TUNE: SONG OF FLIRTATION

Grass on frontier,

Grass on frontier,

When it turns pale, old grow our soldiers here.

The mountains north and south clad in snow white,

For miles and miles shines the moon bright.

Bright is the moon,

Bright is the moon,

Hearing the Tartar horn, the homesick soldiers swoon.

Liu Changqing

TUNE: LAMENT OF A POET

On rippling stream the sinking sun hangs low;

I am grieved to see your lonely boat go.

Birds fly over the plain farther away;

You follow the stream on its eastward way.

Clouds follow you for miles and miles like dream;

The moon sheds light on you up- and down-stream.

How much regret your exile brings, alas!

Just see the gloomy riverside green grass!

Zhang Zhihe

Tune: A Fisherman's Song

In front of western hills white egrets fly up and down,
In peach-mirrored stream mandarin fish are full grown.
In my blue bamboo hat
And green straw cloak, I'd fain
Go fishing careless of slanting wind and fine rain.

Note

Zhang Zhihe (730–782) served in the court as a petty official and then retired to the riverside and lived in seclusion. This poem describing the happiness of a fisherman was wide spread and soon reached Japan. Even the Japanese Emperor (reigned 804–823) wrote five lyrics following the rhyme of his poem.

TUNE: SONG OF FLIRTATION
CLOUDS OF STARS

The Milky Way,
The Milky Way,
Floating over northern town at dawn of day.
I rise and southward gaze, homesick at heart,
For north and south, we're far apart.
Apart we are,
Apart we are.
Beneath the same Milky Way each like a lonely star.

Liu Yuxi

Tune: Dreaming of the Southern Shore

Gone on the wing,

Farewell to lovers of spring!

The willow sways their leaves;

Fair maiden waves her sleeves.

Sweet orchid wet with dew sheds tears to bid adieu.

Sitting alone, could she not frown?

Note

Liu Yuxi (772–842) was well known for his popular songs which depict the life and love of the common people. This song displays a happy combination of natural scenery and inner feeling of the persona.

TUNE: RIVER GODDESSES

River Xiang flows,
River Xiang flows,
Nine cloudy peaks still frown their gloomy brows.
If you ask where are the princesses now, alas!
See autumn weep her dew on withered grass!

TUNE: RIVER GODDESSES

Specked bamboo,
Specked bamboo,
Lovesickness crystallizes drop by drop into rue.
If you would hear the Southern lute sing of their woe,
Wait deep in night when streams with moonlit tears overflow.

Bai Juyi

TUNE: DREAMING OF THE SOUTHERN SHORE

Fair Southern shore,
With scenes I did adore.
At sunrise riverside flowers redder than fire;
In spring green waves grew as blue as sapphire.
How could I not admire?

Note

Bai Juyi (772–846) was a popular realistic poet who served as official in the south of the Yangzi River.

Tune: Dreaming of the Southern Shore

Dreaming of Southern shore,
It's Hangzhou I adore.
The laurels fallen from the moon I'd like to store,
And watch in the pavilion rise the tidal bore.
When can I visit it once more?

Tune: Dreaming of the Southern Shore

Second of all,
I dream of Southern palace hall.
A cup of wine green as bamboo exhaling spring,
Fair dancers two by two like drunken lotus sing.
When can I see them on the wing?

TUNE: EVERLASTING LONGING

See the Bian River flow
And the Si River flow!
By Ancient Ferry, mingling waves, they go,
The Southern hills reflect my woe.

My thought stretches endlessly,
My grief wretches endlessly,
So thus until my husband comes to me,
Alone on moon-lit balcony.

Note

This lyric depicts the longing of a young woman for the return of her husband. Leaning on the railings of a balcony on a moon-lit night, she sees the two rivers meet at the ancient ferry where people used to bid farewell, but where she cannot find her husband home-coming, so she feels the hills there saddened by her grief.

Wen Tingyun

TUNE: BUDDHIST DANCERS

The moonlit balustrades remind her of her dear;

The swaying willow tree cannot retain spring here.

Outdoors spread sad and dreary grass,

His neighing horse not heard, alas!

Golden birds over curtained bed,

From candles burned sad tears are shed.

The cuckoo cries o'er fallen flower;

She wakes from dreams in her green bower.

Note

Wen Tingyun (813–870) was traditionally regarded as the first major lyricist.

Tune: Buddhist Dancers

In jewel case hairpin with golden love-birds seen,
And from her fragrant bower southern mountains green.
Thread by thread hang the willow trees,
The postside bridge in wind and breeze.

No message brought to painted door,
Lush grass outspread on southern shore.
The mirrored faces far apart,
Who knows the lonely longing heart?

TUNE: BUDDHIST DANCERS

In southern garden piled up willow down remains.
How can they bear on mourning day the sudden showers!
The sun declines after the rains,
Fragrant are desolate apricot flowers.

Silent, she remakes up her face,
Her pillow still reveals her bore.
The twilight deepens at slow pace,
Lonely, she leans against the door.

TUNE: BUDDHIST DANCERS

The moon shining in the sky shows it is midnight,
Behind the double screen none to talk with in sight.
A wreath of smoke rises deep in the room;
Not yet undressed, she goes to bed in gloom.

How she regrets the bygone years!
Yet the bygone still reappears.
The waning moon sheds dew on flowers,
Her bed knows chilly morning hours.

TUNE: SONG OF WATERCLOCK

Stars twinkle sparse and few,

Drumbeats and bells not heard,

Beyond the screen the moon wanes with the early bird.

Orchids laden with dew,

'Neath slanting willow trees

In the yard fallen petals piled when blows the breeze.

In her bower still drear,

She leans on balustrade,

Gazing afar, she feels as gloomy as last year.

Again now spring is late,

How she longs for her mate!

The happy time and bygone days like dreams all fade.

TUNE: A SOUTHERN SONG

Golden parrot in hand,
In phoenix dress he stands.
She steals a glance, contemplating without a word.
Why not be wedded to him and be his love bird?

TUNE: DREAMING OF THE SOUTH SHORE

After dressing my hair,
I alone climb the stair.
On the railings I lean,
To view the river scene.
Many sails pass me by,
But not the one for which wait I.
The slanting sun sheds a sympathetic ray,
The carefree river carries it away.
My heart breaks at the sight
Of the islet with duckweed white.

Note

Wen Tingyun's lyrics are richly embellished and full of implicit meaning, but this poem simply narrates in the folk-song manner the sorrow of a young woman who, gazing on the river and the islet where people used to bid farewell, is waiting all day long for the return of her husband.

TUNE: FROM THE RIVER

Unoccupied

By the lakeside,

She gazes on far-flung pathways,

Flowery bridges and beach in rainy haze.

It's a sad sight the songstress fair

Knitting her soft brows cannot bear

All the day long.

How can she forget the evening tidal song?

Where is his boat which has to roam

Far, far from her and far from home?

It is late spring,

And her heart will break to hear orioles sing.

Taking a look,

West of the brook,

At the long willowy pathway,

She cannot hear the horse of the roamer neigh.

Note

This lyric depicts the sorrow of a fair songstress who, gazing in the rain on the pathway where her beloved parted from her, and remembering the evenings they used to spend together, is waiting in vain for his return.

Huangfu Song

TUNE: THE SOUTH RECALLED

Candle-wick burned,
Red cannas painted on the screen dark turned.
I dreamed of mume-fruit rip'ring on the Southern shore,
Of flute-songs played adrift one rainy night of yore,
Of whispers lost
In running stream below the bridge beside the post.

Note

Huangfu Song was one of the precursors of the lyric poets of the "School among Flowers." This lyric describes one of his dreams on a night when the candle-wick was burned out. It reveals his nostalgia for the southern country.

Wei Zhuang

TUNE: BUDDHIST DANCERS

How sad and drear I left the rosy bower at night!
The bed with curtain half rolled up in candlelight.
The waning moon saw me outdoor
Part with the beauty I adore.

My lute adorned with golden bird
Sang on its strings the oriole's word:
O Come back soon to your green bower
To see your beauty like a flower!

Note

Wei Zhuang (836–910) was considered one of the leaders of the "School among Flowers." In contrast to the ornate rhetoric of other lyric poets of this School, his diction is simple and direct and explicit.

TUNE: BUDDHIST DANCERS

All men will say the Southern land is fair,
A wanderer is willing to spend his whole life there.
He'd like to see spring water bluer than the sky
And, listening to rain, in painted ship to lie.

The wine-shop waitress looks like the moon bright,
Like snow or frost congealed her arms are white.
Till he grows old, from South lands he won't part,
To leave this land for home would break his heart.

Note

This lyric is revealed a Northerner's love for the beautiful Southern land.

TUNE: BUDDHIST DANCERS

How fine in Eastern Capital is the spring time!
In alien land old grows its talent in his prime.
Over the principal pool the willows cast their shade,
How could my puzzled mind not fade!

Peach blossoms blend with water green;
Two love-birds on each other lean.
Regret congealed in setting sun,
When can my longing heart be done!

TUNE: ENDLESS AS THE SKY

In scholartree's green shade the golden orioles sing;
The deep courtyard is silent at noonday of spring.
The curtain hanging down,
The phoenix dancing on
The lonely screen by which a stick of incense burns.

The cloud in azure sky
Floats over far and nigh.
Likewise my dreaming soul flies to and fro in vain,
Night after night my window weeps in wind and rain.
Do you believe for you my broken heart ever yearns?

Tune: Cup Made of Lotus Leaf

I still remember that year beneath the flowers
At late hours
When I first came to know you, lady sweet,
West of your poolside bowers,
And hand in hand we promised secretly to meet.

How sad to hear beneath waning moon the orioles cry
When severed you and I!
Since then we're kept apart.
Living in places where none knows our heart,
Never to meet again as you know why.

TUNE: SONG OF WATERCLOCK

Cold drum beats and rings bell,

Dim tower stands with bowers,

The moon shines on the rails around the golden well.

Deep court closed by the wall,

Empty the courtyard small,

Drunken with fragrant dew and paved with fallen flowers.

In mist veiled willow trees,

Spring vapor dims the sight,

The waterside bower drowned in candlelight.

She leans on railings, ill at ease,

Her sleeves are wet with tear on tear,

She's waiting for her love, but he does not appear.

Li Ye

Tune: Buddhist Dancers

Gazing on my former capital from the height,
In boundless sky I only find swallows in flight.
I see the river flow
And mountains high and low.

Trees veiled in mist still sway,
My envoy on the way.
Would he bring heroes here
Help me reign far and near?

Ouyang Jiong

TUNE: SONG OF THE SOUTHERN COUNTRY

The sandy rivershore extends far, far away.

The clouds on our way back are gilt by slanting sun-ray.

By waterside the peacocks preen

Their tails golden or green;

Though startled, they won't stir when passers-by are seen.

TUNE: CALMING THE WAVES

Unoccupied, I see through window screen warm day,
In vernal water of little pool cloud disappears.
Several red crabapple trees will fade away,
How can I bear
To pass in inner room my blooming years!

I lean on my embroidered bed alone and apart,
With broken heart.
On blooming cheek flow down two streams of tears.
So full of care,
The maiden of next door asks when he'll no more roam.
What can I say shame-faced but that he's not yet home?

He Ning

TUNE: SONG OF RIVERSIDE TOWN

The wind blows through groves of bamboo.

Into the door peeps the moon bright.

Playing on zither green

In face of cloudy screen,

I pluck its strings so light,

Afraid not to hear your horse neigh.

Regretful and bashful I say:

Why are you late tonight to our late rendezvous?

TUNE: SONG OF RIVERSIDE TOWN

The waterclock drips when the stars move in the sky.

It is midnight.

Facing the oriole perching high,

Amid flower and flower

I seem to hear your horse trot light.

Smiling, I smooth my robe and open my bower.

Nothing in hand, no one in view,

I go down steps to welcome you.

Niu Qiao

TUNE: BUDDHIST DANCERS

Awake in phoenix-like dancing dress from her dream,

She hears a pair of swallows whisper on the beam.

Outdoors willow downs fly,

Her love has not come nigh.

Powdered face wet with tear,

Eyebrows like spring hills drear.

Where's the far-off frontier?

How long spring days appear!

TUNE: RIVERSIDE DAFFODILS

The waves of Lake Dongting blend with clouds in the sky;
Like wreath of smoke Royal Isle stands,
A real sphere of fairylands.
Jade palace and bowers high
With the bright moon in beauty vie.

For rules and miles cold autumn hue on water spread,
Stars twinkle in the lake as overhead,
Frost-bitten leaves in orange forest look more red.
To the Seventh Celestial Spheres
A hidden way appears.

Gu Xiong

TUNE: WILLOW BRANCH

How lonely do I feel in chilly autumn night!
The waterclock drips long.
I see the incense melt and flicker candlelight,
But hear no lovebirds' song.

I do not know where is roving my gallant fair;
I can find him nowhere.
I only hear banana in the yard complain
About the drizzling rain.

Sun Guangxian

TUNE: FOUNTAIN OF WINE

The boundless desert looked desolate,

Long, long the road to Southern Gate.

Your horse was heard to neigh,

You were seen on your way,

E'en border clouds felt sad.

The sable coat in which you're clad

May be outworn, your uniform too tight,

The thousand-mile northwest frontier with frost is white.

In silk I'm dressed,

But my heart cannot fly

In dreams to the northwest,

So I mount the tower high.

Note

Sun Guangxian (c. 900–968) was a lyric poet of the "School among Flowers." This lyric depicts a young woman recalling her husband parting from her for the Southern Gate in the northwest border, thinking of him when frost falls in the desert, and feeling grieved that she could not go to see him even in her dreams.

TUNE: PAYING HOMAGE TO THE GOLDEN GATE

I could not make him stay.
Even if I could, it would be useless anyway.
I seem to see him still in snowwhite silken gown,
Leaving for Vernal Town.

Of parting he made light.
I'm out of mind, when out of sight.
He sails on the river with all his might.
Though I admire the thirty-six lovebirds in vain,
Still lonely as a swan I remain.

Li Xun

TUNE: CLOUD OVER MOUNT WITCH

The ancient shrine still stands by the green hill;
The wanton palace still by the blue rill.
The beauty's bower sees and hears their song;
The bygone days still haunt my mind for long.

The clouds bring day and night fresh showers;
The mist veils spring and autumn flowers.
Why should the wailing apes come near my lonely boat?
A lonely traveler sees grief enough afloat.

Note

Li Xun was a lyric poet of the "School among Flowers." His lyrics are
full of local colour.

TUNE: SONG OF A SOUTHERN COUNTRY

A skiff goes along
A lotus pond,
Sleeping lovebirds start at oarswomen's song.
Perfumed maidens leaning on each other make fun,
Vying to be the fairest one,
They take round lotus leaves to shun
The setting sun.

TUNE: SONG OF A SOUTHERN COUNTRY

What could I say,
Meeting with thee late on a fine day,
Before the royal terrace under a plane tree?
I stole an amorous glance at thee.
Leaving my hairpin beam,
I rode on elephant and crossed the stream.

TUNE: BUDDHIST DANCERS

The pool is wrinkled by the rising breeze;
The door is closed against blooming plane trees.
The plain drowned in setting sunlight,
A pair of partridges swift in flight.

Where is her roamer's sail?
She longs for him to no avail.
Silent with broken heart in dream,
Awake, she sees but misty stream.

TUNE: BUDDHIST DANCERS

I see in rain a pair of swallows swift in flight,
The fallen petals outspread in deep red or bright..
On strings of precious lute I play;
With his sail my heart s far away.

Beyond the cloud in Southern sky
He stays now a year has passed by.
Incense burned out by painted screen,
Oh, where can my old love be seen?

TUNE: CALMING THE WAVES

I wish to be a hermit under rainbow cloud;

Enjoying lakeside spring, of vain fame I'm not proud.

I sail a leaf like boat and croon my verse while drunk,

White cloud in water sunk,

How happy I will be, from fetters now I'm free!

I love an isle in bloom with gulls as my compeers,

Deep in the rear,

I won't see men from vanity fair all the year.

Having discerning eyes and discerning ears,

Happy at heart,

I'm dressed in lotus leaves, from the world far apart.

TUNE: CALMING THE WAVES

Wild geese pass autumn sky when it is deep at night;
Mist veils the moon and dims the lotus pool in sight.
How could I easily forget the bygone days
Drowned in moonrays!
My man is so far away, still by lakeside he stays.

I weave my lines he may read in order reverse,
But who will send my verse?
Before my mirror I undress my hair in tears.
The incense burned up, cold the gold burner appears.
My sorrow will last long,
Outlasting chirping insects and washerwomen's song.

Feng Yansi

TUNE: MAGPIE ON THE BRANCH

Can melancholy, oh! be laid for long aside?

When comes spring tide,

It will renew.

I'm sick of wine each day with flowers fair in view,

How can a mirrored rosy face not change its hue?

Over the riverside green grass sway willow trees.

I ask why should grief new

Oh! come from year to year.

I stand alone on lonely bridge with sleeves full of breeze,

When men are gone, the wood sees the new moon appear.

Note

Feng Yansi (903–960) was prime minister in the court of the second ruler of the Southern Tang (937–975). His lyrics show the subtle refinement of a courtier.

Tune: Magpie on the Branch

Petals by petals mume blossoms fall from the trees,
Unwilling still,
Whirling like snow in breeze,
Adieu to songstresses and flutists of last night!
Awake from wine, what boundless sorrow left and right!

The tower feels a bitter chill from hill to hill;
Away fly the wild geese,
The evening shrouded in mist far and near,
I lean on balustrade, my love won't reappear.
Longing for him, my kerchief wet with tear on tear.

TUNE: BUTTERFLY IN LOVE WITH FLOWER

How many times in phoenix bower we've drunk our fill!

We meet tonight,

Better than last time when you were in sight.

But whispering past joy, you turn your face away,

Your eyebrows knit look like out-stretched vernal hill.

The candle sheds its tears to hear the flute complain.

You smooth you silk robe long,

And try to sing but feel not gay.

Drunk, we will not refuse to dry our cup again:

Our heart will be broken to hear the parting song.

TUNE: PURE SERENE MUSIC

After the rain mist seems to freeze,
The pool over brimmed with water green.
A pair of swallows fly through weeping willow trees
Before my boudoir with uprolled screen.

At dusk I lean alone on balustrade;
The new moon in the southwest looks like half a ring.
Fallen on marble steps, the petals fade.
How can my silken robe bear the cold spring?

TUNE: PAYING HOMAGE AT THE GOLDEN GATE

The breeze begins to blow
And it ruffles a pool of spring water below.
Crushing pink apricot petals in hand, I play
With a pair of lovebirds on the fragrant pathway.

Seeing ducks fight, alone on the railings I lean,
Slanting upon my head a hairpin of jade green.
Waiting for you the whole day long wears out my eyes,
Raising my head, I'm glad to hear magpies.

Note

In this well-known lyric, Feng Yansi paints a leisure-class lady who has nothing to do all day tong, whose mind is like a pool ruffled by a sudden breeze while waiting for her husband, and who is glad to hear the magpies chatter, which is supposed to announce the expected arrival.

TUNE: LONG-LIVED BEAUTY
THREE WISHES

Feasting in spring,
A cup of wine in hand, I sing,
And with three bows
I make three vows:
I wish you long, long life,
Myself your healthy wife,
And like a pair of swallows on the bream,
We'll share from year to year our joy and dream.

TUNE: JOY OF PLAYING BALL

I've not exhausted yet my joy of wine and song,
And come to linger on the bridge over the stream.
The rippling waves grieve white mume blossoms thereamong,
The breeze invades my silken dress, my heart feels chill.
Think not to go back to your dream!
Enjoy the aftertaste of tonight to the fill!

TUNE: JOY OF PLAYING BALL

After my pleasure seeking in rain, it's not fine;
Heavy wind spreads light mist over grass before my bowers.
The orioles' soft songs pass by sweet flowers,
Drunk, who would listen to an intoxicating song?
I hold up high my cup of wine
To the beloved who will love spring for long.

Li Jing

TUNE: ENDLESS AS THE SKY

Before her mirror where a crescent moon peeps in,
She's too weary to dress her hair with phoenix pin.
From bowers to bowers
Curtains hang down with ease;
She's grieved to see flowers
Wafting in the breeze.

Dreaming of willow banks green with sweet grass,
She wakes to find no golden well with its windlass.
Sobered from wine at the dead of night still,
She feels more sad with spring than ill.

TUNE: GAZING AFAR

Bright flowers on the steps of jade

Look like brocade,

The crimson doorway

Oft closed all day.

The cold won't leave when night is deep.

How can I fall asleep?

From the censer of gold

Rises wreath on wreath of smoke cold.

Under the waning moon the washerwomen who pound

Bring no message but a longing sound.

The golden windows suddenly start

My longing heart.

When you come back from far away,

My hair will have turned grey.

TUNE: SILK-WASHING STREAM

My hands have rolled pearl-screens up to their jade hooks.
Locked in my bower as before, how sad spring looks!
Who is reigning over flowers wafting in the breeze?
I brood over it without cease.

Blue birds bring no news from beyond the cloud; in vain
The lilac blossoms knot my sorrow in the rain.
I look back on green waves in twilight far and nigh:
They roll on as far as the sky.

TUNE: SILK-WASHING STREAM

The lotus flowers fade with blue-black leaves decayed;
The west wind ripples and saddens the water green
As time wrinkles a fair face.
Oh, how can it bear
To be seen, to be seen!

In the fine rain she dreams of the far-off frontiers;
Her bower's cold with music played on flute of jade.
Oh, with how much regret and with how many tears
She leans on balustrade!

Li Yu

TUNE: SILK-WASHING STREAM

Above the thirty-foot-high flagpole shines the sun;
Incense is added to gold burners one by one;
Red carpets wrinkle as each dancing step is done.

Fair dancers let gold hairpins drop with rhythm fleet;
Drunk, maidens oft inhale the smell of flowers sweet;
From hall to hall flute's heard to play and drum to beat.

Note

Li Yu (937–978) was the last ruler of the Southern Tang. In 975, his capital fell and he himself was taken captive. In his captivity he wrote many of his best lyrics which represent the highest achievement of the lyric poets of that period.

TUNE: A CASKET OF PEARLS

Donning her evening dress, she drips
Some drops of sandalwood stain on her lips,
Which, cherry-red, suddenly open flung,
Reveal her tiny clovelike tongue,
She sings a song in her voice clear.

Careless about her gauze sleeves soiled with crimson stain,
She fills her cup with fragrant wine again.
Drunken and indolent, she leans across her bed,
And chewing bits of bastings red.
She spits them with a smile upon her master dear.

TUNE: SPRING IN JADE PAVILION

In spring the palace maids line up row after row,

Their evening dress revealing their skin bright as snow.

The tunes they play on the flutes reach the waves and cloud;

With songs of "Rainbow Dress" once more the air is loud.

Who wants to spread more fragrance before fragrant spring?

When drunk, I beat on rails as vibrates my heartstring.

Don't light on my returning way a candle red!

I'd like to see the hoofs reflect moonlight they tread.

TUNE: BUDDHIST DANCERS

Enjoy a vernal day ere it passes away;
Admire the lovely flowers at their loveliest hours!
Drink cups of wine undistilled,
By white jadelike hands filled!

Why not make merry while we may?
In royal garden spring will longer stay,
We drink, talk freely and complete
Our verse as drums begin to beat.

TUNE: BUDDHIST DANCERS

Bright flowers bathed in thin mist and dim moonlight,
'Tis best time to steal out to see my love tonight.
With stocking feet on fragrant steps I tread,
Holding in hand my shoes sown with gold thread.

We meet south of the painted hall,
And trembling in his arms I fall.
"It's hard for me to come o'er here,
So you may love your fill, my dear!"

TUNE: BUDDHIST DANCERS

An angel's kept secluded in the fairy hill;
She naps in painted hall, so quiet and so still.
Beside the pillow spreads her cloudlike hair pell-mell;
Her broidered dress exhales an exotic sweet smell.

I come in stealth and click the locked pearly door,
Awaking her behind the screen from lovely dreams.
I can't get in but gaze at her face I adore;
She smiles at me, her eyes send out amorous beams.

TUNE: BUDDHIST DANCERS

The crisp bamboo with brass reeds tinkles in cold air;
New music is slowly played by her fingers fair.
In secret we exchange amorous looks;
Like autumn waves desire o'erflows its nooks.

Clouds bring fresh showers for the thirsting flowers
And gratify the sweet desire of ours.
After the feast all vanishes, it seems;
Still is my soul enchant'd in vernal dreams.

Tune: Migrant Orioles

The morning moon is sinking;
Few clouds are floating there.
I lean oft on my pillow with no word.
E'en in my dream I'm thinking
Of the green grass so fair,
But no wild geese afar are heard.

No more orioles' song,
Late vernal blooms whirl round.
In courtyard as in painted hall
Solitude reigns the whole night long.
Don't sweep away the fallen petals on the ground!
Leave them there till the dancer comes back from the ball!

TUNE: SONG OF PICKING MULBERRIES

Red blooms are driven down by the departing spring,
Dancing while lingering.
Though in the drizzling rain
I try to unknit my eyebrows, they're knit again.

No message comes to lonely windows all the day,
The incense burned to ashes grey,
How can I from spring thoughts be free?
I try to sleep, but in my dream spring comes to me.

TUNE: EVERLASTING LONGING

Her cloudlike hair
With jade hairpin,
In dress so fair
Of gauze so thin,
Lightly she knits her brows dark green.

In autumn breeze
And autumn rain,
Lonely banana trees
Tremble outside the window screen.
Oh! How to pass a long, long night again!

Tune: A Fisherman's Song

White-crested waves aspire to a skyful of snow;
Spring displays silent peach and plum trees in a row.
A fishing rod,
A pot of wine,
Who in this world can boast of happier life than mine?

Tune: A Fisherman's Song

The dripping oar, the vernal wind, a leaflike boat,
A light fishhook, a silken thread of fishing line,
An islet in flowers,
A bowl of wine,
Upon the endless waves with full freedom I float.

Tune: Gratitude for New Bounties

In our pavilion my flutist can't be found,

Leaving the scene of royal garden unenjoyed,

The pink and golden flowers nodding to the ground.

By the east wind I feel annoyed;

It brings but half spring fragrance round.

The dreaming window keeps the sun's departing rays,

How I regret those bygone days!

With railings green a weeping willow plays,

We met only to part;

It's like a dream in vain to keep in heart.

TUNE: GRATITUDE FOR NEW BOUNTIES

On moonlit steps, oh, all
The cherry blossoms fall.
Lounging upon her ivory bed, she looks sad
For the same regret this day last year she had.

Like languid cloud looks her dishevelled head;
With tears is wet her corset red.
For whom is she lovesick?
Drunk, she dreams with the window curtain thick.

TUNE: GRATITUDE OR NEW BOUNTIES

The courtyard is deserted when the guests are gone;

I'm left alone,

The painted hall half veiled by pearly screen.

A gentle breeze blows from the woods on a night tender;

As I turn back, a crescent moon so slender

Over my little tower can be seen.

Though spring still reigns, man will grow old in vain.

How long

Will sorrow old and new remain?

Behind the golden window I feel weary;

Awake, I still feel drowsy and dreary,

But my drunk face is gladdened by a flutist's song.

TUNE: GRATITUDE FOR NEW BOUNTIES

All cherry blossoms fallen, weary will be spring,

Coming back, I pass by your swing.

The hidden waterclock still punctuates late hours;

The slanting moon sheds light on the branches with flowers.

... ...

Under your window I am waiting all night long.

But have you heard my heart sing its love song?

Tune: Gratitude for New Bounties

Who could retain the autumn light fading away?

At dusk the marble steps are strewn with withered leaves.

The Double Ninth Day comes again;

The view from terrace and pavilion grieves.

Fragrance of dogwood spray

And smell of violet flowers

Waft in courtyards and bowers

Veiled in the grizzling mist and drizzling rain.

New-come wild geese cackle old songs chilly and drear.

Why should my longing look alike from year to year?

TUNE: THE LOVER'S RETURN

Beyond wind-rippled water hills swallow the sun;

Spring's come, still nothing can be done.

Fallen blooms run riot; wine drunk,

Drowned in flute songs, in dream the princess is sunk.

Without a word.

No tinkling heard,

Her evening dress undone.

For whom has she to dress her hair?

With fleeting time will fade the fair.

Alone she leans on rails before the dying sun.

TUNE: BUTTERFLIES IN LOVE WITH FLOWERS

In long long night by waterside I stroll with ease.
Having just passed the Mourning Day,
Again I mourn for spring passing away.
A few raindrops fall and soon
They're held off by the breeze.
The floating clouds veil and unveil the dreaming moon.

Peach and plum blossoms can't retain the dying spring.
Who would sit on the swing,
Smiling and whispering?
Does she need a thousand outlets for her heart
So as to play on earth its amorous part?

TUNE: SONG OF THE WASHERWOMAN

Deep garden still,
Small courtyard void.
The intermittent beetles chill
And intermittent breezes trill.
What can I do with sleep destroyed
But count the sound, in endless night,
Brought through the lattice window by moonlight?

TUNE: SONG OF THE WASHERWOMAN

Disheveled cloudlike hair,
The evening dress undone,
Like distant hills arch the frowning brows of the fair one.
Her fragrant cheeks lean to one side
Against her tender hands.
For whom glisten her tears undried?
Against the balustrade she stands.

Tune: Pure Serene Music

Spring has half gone since we two parted;
I can see nothing now but broken-hearted.
Mume blossoms fall below the steps like whirling snow;
They cover me still though brushed off a while ago.

No message comes from the wild geese's song;
In dreams you cannot come back for the road is long.
The grief of separation like spring grass
Grows each day you're farther away, alas!

Tune: Song of Picking Mulberries

Beside the windlassed well at dusk the lonesome trees
Are trembling in the autumn breeze.
A shower brings new sorrow;
The hooked curtain hangs up, waiting for the morrow.

She frowns before the window at departing spring,
Her longing on the wing.
She'd send to him her dream;
The winding river's cold waves won't bear it upstream.

Tune: Immortals at the River

All cherries fallen, gone is spring;
The golden butterflies waft on the wing.
West of the bower at the moon the cuckoo cries;
The screen of pearls sees dreary evening smoke rise.

Loneliness reigns behind the closed door
When the court is no more.
I gaze on mist-veiled grass.
When may I come back to hear my steed neigh? Alas!
The willow down clings to the screen, it seems.
My soul could only come back in dreams.

Tune: Crows Crying at Night

Wind blew and rain fell all night long;
Curtains and screens rustled like autumn song.
The water clock drip-dropping and the candle dying,
I lean on pillow restless, sitting up or lying.

All are gone with the running stream;
My floating life is but a dream.
Let wine cups be my surest haunt!
On nothing else now can I count.

Tune: The Beautiful Lady Yu

The vernal breeze returns, my small courtyard turns green;

Again the budding willows bring back spring. I lean

Alone on rails for long without a word.

As in the bygone years the crescent moon in seen

And songs of flute are heard.

The banquet not yet closed, music floats in the air;

Ice on the pond begins to melt.

In deep painted hall with candles bright, dim perfume's smelt.

The thought of age snowing white hair

On my forehead is hard to bear.

TUNE: DANCE OF THE CAVALRY

A reign of forty years
O'er a land of three thousand li,
My royal palaces touching the celestial spheres,
My shady forest looking like a hazy sea.
What did I know of shields and spears?

A captive now, I'm worn away,
Thinner I grow, my hair turns gray.
O how could I forget the hurried parting day
When by the band the farewell songs were played
And I shed tears before my palace maid!

Note

In this lyric we find a sharp contrast between the past in the first stanza and the present in the second.

TUNE: GAZING ON THE SOUTHERN SHORE

My idle dream goes far:
In fragrant spring the southern countries are.
Sweet music from the boats on the green river floats;
Fine dust and willow down run riot in the town.
It is the busy hours for admirers of flowers.

TUNE: GAZING ON THE SOUTHERN SHORE

My idle dream goes far:
In autumn clear the southern countries are.
For miles and miles a stretch of hills in chilly hue,
Amid the reeds is moored a lonely boat in view.
In moonlit tower a flute is played for you.

TUNE: DREAMING ON THE SOUTHERN SHORE

How much regret
In last night's dream!
It seemed as if we were in royal garden yet:
Dragon like steeds and carriages run like flowing stream;
In vernal wind the moon and flowers beam.

TUNE: DREAMING ON THE SOUTHERN SHORE

How many tears
Crisscross my cheeks between my ears!
Don't ask about my grief of recent years
Nor play on flute when tears come out,
Or else my heart would break, no doubt!

TUNE: CROWS CRYING AT NIGHT

Spring's rosy colour fades from forest flowers
Too soon, too soon.
How can they bear cold morning showers
And winds at noon!

Your rouged tears like crimson rain
Intoxicate my heart.
When shall we meet again?
As water eastward flows, so shall we part.

Note

The image of crimson flowers falling in the cold morning rain is compared to the rouged tears of a beautiful woman the poet is going to leave. Through this image he conveys the idea that even the external world shares his personal sorrow.

TUNE: CROWS CRYING AT NIGHT

Silent, I go up to the west tower alone
And see the hooklike moon.
The plane trees lonesome and drear
Lock in the courtyard autumn clear.

Cut, it won't break;
Ruled, it will make
A mess to wake
An unspeakable taste in the heart.
Such is the grief to part.

Note

This is one of the best lyrics describing the sorrow of separation. We can find that after an implicit description of his loneliness in the first stanza, the poet utters three short lines mirroring the intensity of his sorrow and then the final line revealing the relaxation of his feeling.

TUNE: MIDNIGHT SONG

From sorrow and regret our life cannot be free.
Why is this soul-consuming grief e'er haunting me!
I went to my lost land in dreams;
Awake, I find tears flow in streams.

Who would ascend with me those towers high?
I can't forget fine autumn days gone by.
Vain is the happiness of yore;
It melts like dream and is no more.

Tune: Ripples Sifting Sand

It saddens me to think of days gone by,
With old familiar scenes in my mind's eye.
The autumn wind is blowing hard
O'er moss-grown steps in deep courtyard.
Let beaded screen hang idly unrolled at the door.
Who will come any more?

Sunk and buried my golden armour lies;
Amid o'ergrowing weeds my vigour dies.
The blooming moon is rising in the evening sky.
The palaces of jade
With marble balustrade
Are reflected in vain on the River Qinhuai.

Tune: The Beautiful Lady Yu

When will there be no more an autumn moon and spring time flowers

For me who had so many memorable hours?

My attic which last night in the east wind did stand

Reminds me cruelly of the lost moonlit land.

Carved balustrades and marble steps must still be there,

But rosy faces cannot be as fair.

If you would ask me how my sorrow has increased,

Just see the over-brimming river flowing east!

Note

This is supposed to be the last lyric written by Li Yu before his death. As John Mill says, "all poetry is of the nature of soliloquy." "The peculiarity of poetry appears to us to lie in the poet's utter unconsciousness of a listener." Unfortunately, the emperor of Song "overheard" this poem and ordered the poet to take poison. So it may well be said that this lyric epitomizes Nietzsche's concept that all literature must be written in blood.

Tune: Ripples Sifting Sand

The curtain cannot keep out the patter of rain,
Springtime is on the wane.
In the deep of the night my quilt is not cold-proof.
Forgetting I am under hospitable roof,
Still in my dream I seek for pleasures vain.

Don't lean alone on the railings and
Yearn for the boundless land!
To bid farewell is easier than to meet again.
With flowers fallen on the waves spring's gone amain,
So is the paradise of men.

Note

This is one of the best lyrics written by Li Yu after he was taken as a captive north to the Song capital. Fallen flowers, rolling waves, departing spring, all reminded him of his lost country.

Anonymous

TUNE: BACKYARD FEAST

My homeland thousand miles away,

My bower left ten years ago,

My soul can't fly o'er streams and mountains e'en in dreams.

Unpenciled brows and oldened eyes can't bear spring day;

My fragrance fades like jade, only my mirrors know.

Swallows come back in pair

Should know smiling despair.

Nor dance nor song

Regret clear river long.

Green leaves from thousand trees outspread,

A yard of fallen petals red.

许译中国经典诗文集

唐五代词选

许渊冲　译

五洲传播出版社　中华书局

　　《中国词选》罗马尼亚译者说："中国词使我们认
识了一个无容置疑的充满魅力、抒情性强和意境深邃的世
界，在这个世界里洋溢着书面上看到的花朵的香气"，中
国的词"是三千多年悠久文化与文明的结晶"[①]。

　　中国词的兴起，可以追溯到隋代。著名的《河传》、
《柳枝》就是当时的民歌，《水调》也是开凿运河的产
物。到了唐代，词有了新的发展。1900年在敦煌发现的唐
人曲词残卷，共有1160余首，其中多数来自民间，有鲜明
的性格特征和浓厚的生活气息，如《菩萨蛮》：

　　　　枕前发尽千般愿：要休且待青山烂。

　　　　水面上秤锤浮，直待黄河彻底枯。

　　　　白日参辰现，北斗回南面。

　　　　休即未能休，且待三更见日头。

　　这首词写爱情的盟誓，充满了坚贞的信念，火一样
的热情，新颖泼辣，奇特生动。就形式而言，第三句中的
"上"字和第四句、第八句中的"直待"、"且待"，都
是衬字。如果把衬字取消，形式就和其他《菩萨蛮》的曲
调一致了。此外，《菩萨蛮》的调名也说明了佛教对唐代
文化的影响。

　　这本词集里选了一些唐代民间词，《鹊踏枝》通过
妇人和灵鹊的对话，写出了妇人对和平幸福生活的热烈向
往，表现手法相当新颖灵活，语言也活泼生动。此外，

---

① 转引自1981年2月1日《人民日报》。

《鹊踏枝》的调名也说明了，词的内容和调名最初是有关系的。

文人词里最早的作品，据传是李白的《菩萨蛮》和《忆秦娥》，但也有人认为这两首词都是后来无名词人写的。《菩萨蛮》一词据说"写在鼎州沧水驿楼"，"解者或依此，以为既写在驿楼，当即在驿楼中所作。既驿楼中作，当即为男子自己抒怀乡之情，故定此词的主人公是男子"①。但是靳极苍说："就词本身来看，还是解作闺情，定主人公为怀远盼归的少妇为好。"我在这里译成"闺情"。

《忆秦娥》一词，靳极苍说："作者借秦娥的忆旧，以抒发自己伤逝的感情。"李汉超却在《论李白〈忆秦娥〉》②一文中说："年年伤别"，"实指徭戍行人"，因此认为这词是"一首以天宝之乱为背景、充满政治激情的反映唐代由盛转衰的伤时之作。"加上《忆秦娥》的调名与词的内容有关，可能是最初的作品，因此他认为这词不是后人伪作。我觉得他的话很有道理，也在英文注中作了说明。

唐代文人的理想，不是在朝为官，就是在野为民，过隐居的渔樵生活。这种理想反映在词中的，有张志和的《渔父》。这首词的内容和调名一致，被誉为"风流千古"，在当时影响很大，和者如林，很快就传到了日本。据《日本填词学史话》的记载，嵯峨天皇（公元804—823年在位）还曾亲和了五首。

后来，刘禹锡、白居易也相继作词。刘禹锡模仿四

---

① 见靳极苍《唐宋词百首详解》，下同。
② 见《文学评论》1983年第4期。

川民歌，写了一组有名的《竹枝词》。他的《浪淘沙》写妇女结伴到沙滩淘金，内容和调名相关，形式却与后来的《浪淘沙》不同，反而跟七言绝句相近。由此也可看出，词体的形成实源自民歌和绝句[①]。经过刘、白等文人提倡，词逐渐从民间文学的地位登上了文坛。

到了晚唐，涌现出了一批以填词为主要表现手段的艺术家，其中以皇甫松、温庭筠等最为著名。温庭筠作品比较多，词的形式格律到他手里才逐渐完善起来。温庭筠改变了民间词朴素的风格，特别注重修辞的华丽。如《更漏子》：

柳丝长，春雨细，花外漏声迢递。
惊塞雁，起城乌，画屏金鹧鸪。

香雾薄，透帘幕，惆怅谢家池阁。
红烛背，绣帘垂，梦长君不知。

这是一首描写深夜失眠的妇女思念情人的词，写得隐微曲折，婉约含蓄，不好翻译。这里选译了他一首《梦江南》，其中"一切景语"都是"情语"。

温庭筠是"花间派"的代表作家，韦庄和温庭筠齐名，并称"温韦"。温庭筠的风格和李商隐相近，韦庄的风格和白居易相近。韦词浅显如话，富有民间气息，例如他追念为王建夺去的宠姬而作的《女冠子》：

四月十七，正是去年今日。
别君时，忍泪伴低面，含羞半敛眉。

不知魂已断，空有梦相随。
除却天边月，没人知。

_____

① 据刘永济《唐五代两宋词简析》总论。

105

夏承焘认为韦庄词的最大特点，"是把当时文人词带回到民间作品的抒情道路上来"，"影响了后来的李煜、苏轼、辛弃疾诸大家"[①]。

其他"花间派"的词人，夏承焘认为他们共同的特点是："华丽的字面，婉约的表达手法，集中来写女性的美貌和服饰以及她们的离愁别恨。"这里选译了一些风格不同的词，比如李珣所写具有浓厚南方乡土色彩的《南乡子》，以及孙光宪刻划塞外荒凉图景的《酒泉子》。

"花间派"的作者大都是西蜀词人。在晚唐五代与西蜀词并峙的，还有长江下游的另一个词派——南唐词。冯延巳与韦庄分据吴蜀词坛。冯词"所以娱宾而遣兴也"[②]，对北宋词坛影响很大。刘熙载《艺概》中说："冯延巳词，晏同叔（晏殊）得其俊，欧阳永叔（欧阳修）得其深。"冯词和欧词风格近似，有时难分彼此，如《蝶恋花》（庭院深深）一词，就既见于冯词集，又见于欧词集。"庭院深深"，夏承焘说是指一个贵族少妇的深闺，靳极苍却说是指"歌楼妓馆"，靳说更合逻辑。

五代词的代表作家，是南唐后主李煜。"李煜词改革'花间派'涂饰、雕琢的流弊，用清丽的语言、白描的手法和高度的艺术概括力，抓住自己生活感受中最深刻的方面，动人地把情感表达出来，给人深刻的艺术感受"[③]。王国维在《人间词话》中说："温飞卿（温庭筠）之词，句秀也；韦端己（韦庄）之词，骨秀也；李重光（李煜）之词，神秀也。词至李后主而眼界始大，感慨遂深，遂变伶工之词而为士大夫之词。"又说："词人者，不失其赤

---

①③见夏承焘《唐宋词欣赏》。
②见陈世修为冯延巳《阳春集》作的序。

子之心者也。故生于深宫之中，长于妇人之手，是后主为人君所短处，亦即为词人所长处。客观之诗人不可不多阅世，阅世愈深则材料愈丰富，愈变化，《水浒传》、《红楼梦》之作者是也。主观之诗人不必多阅世，阅世愈浅则性情愈真，李后主是也。尼采谓一切文学，余爱以血书者。后主之词。真所谓以血书者也。"这里选译了几乎全部李煜词，其中《乌夜啼》（林花谢了）一首，美国耶鲁大学教授孙康宜认为词人把"春红"、"寒雨"和"胭脂泪"相比，有独到见解，我的译文采用了孙说。

许渊冲
1985年12月于北京大学

敦煌曲子词

凤归云

闺怨

征夫数载，
萍寄他邦。
去便无消息，
累换星霜。
月下愁听砧杵起，
塞燕南行。
孤眠鸾帐里，
枉劳魂梦，
夜夜飞扬。

想君薄行，
更不思量。
谁为传书与，
表妾衷肠？
倚牖无言垂血泪，
暗祝三光。
万般无奈处，
一炉香尽，
又更添香。

抛球乐

怨妇曲

珠泪纷纷湿绮罗，
少年公子负恩多。
当初姊姊分明道：
莫把真心过与他！
子细思量着，
淡薄知闻解好么？

菩萨蛮

千般愿

枕前发尽千般愿，
要休且待青山烂。
水面上秤锤浮，
直待黄河彻底枯。

白日参辰现，
北斗回南面。
休即未能休，
且待三更见日头。

菩萨蛮

边塞词

敦煌古往出神将，
感得诸蕃遥钦仰。
效节望龙庭，
麟台早有名。

只恨隔蕃部，
情恳难申吐。
早晚灭狼蕃，
一齐拜圣颜。

浣溪沙

船夫曲

五里滩头风欲平，
张帆举棹觉船轻。
柔橹不施停却棹，
是船行。

满眼风波多闪灼，
看山恰似走来迎。
子细看山山不动，
是船行。

望江南

临池柳

莫攀我，
攀我太心偏。
我是曲江临池柳，
者人折了那人攀。
恩爱一时间。

望江南

弃妇曲

天上月，
遥望似一团银。
夜久更阑风渐紧，
为奴吹散月边云，
照见负心人。

定风波

书与剑

攻书学剑能几何？
争如沙塞骋偻㑩！
手执绿沉枪似铁，
明月，
龙泉三尺斩新磨。

堪羡昔时军伍，
谩夸儒士德能多，
四塞忽闻狼烟起，
问儒士，
谁人敢去定风波？

鹊踏枝

笼中鸟

叵耐灵鹊多谩语，
送喜何曾有凭据？
几度飞来活捉取，
锁上金笼休共语。

比拟好心来送喜，
谁知锁我在金笼里。
欲她征夫早归来，
腾身却放我向青云里！

南歌子

妻答夫

自从君去后，
无心恋别人。
梦中面上指痕新。
罗带同心自绾，
被猕儿踏破裙。

蝉鬓珠帘乱，
金钗旧股分。
红妆垂泪哭郎君。
信是南山松柏，
无心恋别人。

李白

菩萨蛮

平林漠漠烟如织，
寒山一带伤心碧。
暝色入高楼，
有人楼上愁。

玉阶空伫立，
宿鸟归飞急。
何处是归程？
长亭更短亭。

忆秦娥

箫声咽，
秦娥梦断秦楼月。
秦楼月，
年年柳色，
灞陵伤别。

乐游原上清秋节，
咸阳古道音尘绝。
音尘绝，
西风残照，
汉家陵阙。

戴叔伦

调笑令

边草，边草，
边草尽来兵老。
山南山北雪晴，
千里万里月明。
明月，明月，
胡笳一声愁绝。

刘长卿

谪仙怨

晴川落日初低，
惆怅孤舟解携。
鸟向平芜远近，
人随流水东西。

白云千里万里，
明月前溪后溪。
独恨长沙谪去，
江潭春草萋萋。

渔父

西塞山前白鹭飞，
桃花流水鳜鱼肥。
青箬笠，绿蓑衣，
斜风细雨不须归。

调笑令

河汉

河汉，河汉，
晓挂秋城漫漫。
愁人起望乡思，
江南塞北别离。
离别，离别，
河汉虽同路绝。

刘禹锡

梦江南

春去也，
多谢洛城人。
弱柳从风疑举袂，
从兰裛露似沾巾。
独坐亦含嚬。

潇湘神

湘水流，湘水流，
九疑云物至今愁。
若问二妃何处所，
零陵香草露中秋。

潇湘神

斑竹枝，斑竹枝，
泪痕点点寄相思。
楚客欲听瑶瑟怨，
潇湘深夜月明时。

白居易

忆江南

江南好，
风景旧曾谙。
日出江花红胜火，
春来江水绿如蓝。
能不忆江南？

忆江南

江南忆，
最忆是杭州。
山寺月中寻桂子，
郡亭枕上看潮头。
何日更重游？

忆江南

江南忆，
其次忆吴宫。
吴酒一杯春竹叶，
吴娃双舞醉芙蓉。
早晚复相逢？

长相思

汴水流，
泗水流，
流到瓜洲古渡头。
吴山点点愁。

思悠悠，
恨悠悠，
恨到归时方始休。
月明人倚楼。

温庭筠

菩萨蛮

玉楼明月长相忆，
柳丝袅娜春无力。
门外草萋萋，
送君闻马嘶。

画罗金翡翠，
香烛销成泪。
花落子规啼，
绿窗残梦迷。

菩萨蛮

宝函钿雀金鹨鹏，
沉香阁上吴山碧。
杨柳又如丝，
驿桥春雨时。

画楼音信断，
芳草江南岸。
鸾镜与花枝，
此情谁得知？

菩萨蛮

南园满地堆轻絮，
愁闻一霎清明雨。
雨后却斜阳，
杏花零落香。

无言匀睡脸，
枕上屏山掩。
时节欲黄昏，
无聊独倚门。

菩萨蛮

夜来皓月才当午，
重帘悄悄无人语。
深处麝烟长，
卧时留薄妆。

当年还自惜，
往事那堪忆？
花露月明残，
锦衾知晓寒。

更漏子

星斗稀，钟鼓歇，
帘外晓莺残月。
兰露重，柳风斜，
满庭堆落花。

虚阁上，倚阑望，
还是去年惆怅。
春欲暮，思无穷，
旧欢如梦中。

南歌子

手里金鹦鹉，
胸前绣凤凰。
偷眼暗形相。
不如从嫁与，
作鸳鸯。

梦江南

梳洗罢，
独倚望江楼。
过尽千帆皆不是，
斜晖脉脉水悠悠，
肠断白蘋洲。

河传

湖上，闲望。
雨潇潇，
烟浦花桥路遥。
谢娘翠蛾愁不销，
终朝。
梦魂迷晚潮。

荡子天涯归棹远。
春已晚，
莺语空肠断。
若耶溪，溪水西。
柳堤，
不闻郎马嘶。

忆江南

兰烬落，
屏上暗红蕉。
闲梦江南梅熟日，
夜船吹笛雨萧萧，
人语驿边桥。

韦庄

菩萨蛮

红楼别夜堪惆怅，
香灯半卷流苏帐。
残月出门时，
美人和泪辞。

琵琶金翠羽，
弦上黄莺语。
劝我早归家，
绿窗人似花。

菩萨蛮

人人尽说江南好，
游人只合江南老。
春水碧于天，
画船听雨眠。

垆边人似月，
皓腕凝霜雪。
未老莫还乡，
还乡须断肠。

菩萨蛮

洛阳城里春光好，
洛阳才子他乡老。
柳暗魏王堤，
此时心转迷。

桃花春水渌，
水上鸳鸯浴。
凝恨对残晖，
忆君君不知。

应天长

绿槐荫里黄莺语，
深院无人春昼午。
画帘垂，金凤舞，
寂寞绣屏香一炷。

碧天云，无尽处，
空有梦魂来去。
夜夜绿窗风雨，
断肠君信否？

荷叶杯

记得那年花下，
深夜，初识谢娘时。
水堂西面画帘垂，
携手暗相期。

惆怅晓莺残月，
相别，从此隔音尘。
如今俱是异乡人，
相见更无因。

更漏子

钟鼓寒，楼阁暝，
月照古铜金井。
深院闭，小庭空，
落花香露红。

烟柳重，春雾薄，
灯背水窗高阁。
闲倚户，暗沾衣，
待郎郎不归。

李晔

菩萨蛮

登楼遥望秦宫殿,
茫茫只见双飞燕,
渭水一条流,
千山与万丘。

远烟笼碧树,
陌上行人去。
何处有英雄?
迎归大内中。

南乡子

岸远沙平，
日斜归路晚霞明。
孔雀自怜金翠尾，
临水，
认得行人惊不起。

定风波

暖日闲窗映碧纱，
小池春水浸晴霞。
数树海棠红欲尽，争忍？
玉闺深掩过年华。

独凭绣床方寸乱，肠断。
泪珠穿破脸边花。
邻舍女郎相借问，音信，
教人羞道未还家。

和凝

江城子

竹里风生月上门。
理秦筝，对云屏。
轻拨朱弦，
恐乱马嘶声。
含恨含娇独自语：
今夜约，太迟生。

江城子

斗转星移玉漏频。
已三更，对栖莺。
历历花间，
似有马蹄声，
含笑整衣开绣户，
斜敛手，下阶迎。

菩萨蛮

舞裙香暖金泥凤，
画梁语燕惊残梦。
门外柳花飞，
玉郎犹未归。

愁匀红粉泪，
眉剪春山翠。
何处是辽阳？
锦屏春昼长。

牛希济

临江仙

洞庭波浪飐晴天，
君山一点凝烟，
此中真境属神仙。
玉楼珠殿，
相映月轮边。

万里平湖秋色冷，
星辰垂影参然。
橘林霜重更红艳。
罗浮山下，
有路暗相连。

杨柳枝

秋夜香闺思寂寥，
漏迢迢。
鸳帏罗幌麝烟销，
烛光摇。

正忆玉郎游荡去，
无寻处。
更闻帘外雨潇潇，
滴芭蕉。

孙光宪

酒泉子

空碛无边，
万里阳关道路。
马萧萧，人去去，
陇云愁。

香貂旧制戎衣窄，
胡霜千里白。
绮罗心，魂梦隔，
上高楼。

谒金门

留不得！
留得也应无益。
白纻春衫如雪色，
扬州初去日。

轻别离，
甘抛掷，
江上满帆风疾。
却羡彩鸳三十六，
孤鸾还一只。

巫山一段云

古庙依青嶂，
行宫枕碧流。
水声山色锁妆楼，
往事思悠悠。

云雨朝还暮，
烟花春复秋。
啼猿何必近孤舟？
行客自多愁。

南乡子

乘彩舫，过莲塘，
棹歌惊起睡鸳鸯。
游女带花偎伴笑，
争窈窕，
竞折团荷遮晚照。

南乡子

相见处，晚晴天，
刺桐花下越台前。
暗里回眸深属意，
遗双翠。
骑象背人先过水。

菩萨蛮

回塘风起波纹细，
刺桐花里门斜闭。
残日照平芜，
双双飞鹧鸪。

征帆何处客？
相见还相隔。
不语欲魂消，
望中烟水遥。

菩萨蛮

隔帘微雨双飞燕，
砌花零落红深浅。
捻得宝筝调，
心随征棹遥。

楚天云外路，
动便经年去。
香断画屏深，
旧欢何处寻？

定风波

志在烟霞慕隐沦，
功成归看五湖春。
一叶舟中吟复醉，云水。
此时方认自由身。

花岛为邻鸥作侣，深处。
经年不见市朝人。
已得希夷微妙旨，潜喜。
荷衣蕙带绝纤尘。

定风波

雁过秋空夜未央，
隔窗烟月锁莲塘。
往事岂堪容易想？惆怅。
故人迢递在潇湘。

纵有回文重叠意，谁寄？
解鬟临镜泣残妆。
沉水香消金鸭冷，愁永。
候虫声接杵声长。

鹊踏枝

谁道闲情抛弃久?
每到春来,
惆怅还依旧,
日日花前常病酒,
不辞镜里朱颜瘦。

河畔青芜堤上柳,
为问新愁,
何事年年有?
独立小桥风满袖,
平林新月人归后。

鹊踏枝

梅落繁枝千万片，
犹自多情，
学雪随风转。
昨夜笙歌容易散，
酒醒添得愁无限。

楼上春山寒四面，
过尽征鸿，
暮景烟深浅。
一晌凭栏人不见，
鲛绡掩泪思量遍。

蝶恋花

几度凤楼同饮宴。
此夕相逢，
却胜当时见。
低语前欢频转面，
双眉敛恨春山远。

蜡烛泪流羌笛怨。
偷整罗衣，
欲唱情犹懒。
醉里不辞金爵满，
阳关一曲肠千断。

清平乐

雨晴烟晚，
绿水新池满。
双燕飞来垂柳院，
小阁画帘高卷。

黄昏独倚朱阑，
西南新月眉弯。
砌下落花风起，
罗衣特地春寒。

谒金门

风乍起，
吹绉一池春水。
闲引鸳鸯芳径里，
手挼红杏蕊。

斗鸭阑干独倚，
碧玉搔头斜坠。
终日望君君不至，
举头闻鹊喜。

长命女

陈三愿

春日宴，
绿酒一杯歌一遍。
再拜陈三愿：
一愿郎君千岁，
二愿妾身长健，
三愿如同梁上燕，
岁岁长相见。

抛球乐

酒罢歌余兴未阑，
小桥流水共盘桓。
波摇梅蕊当心白，
风入罗衣贴体寒。
且莫思归去，
须尽笙歌此夕欢。

抛球乐

逐胜归来雨未晴，
楼前风重草烟轻。
谷莺语软花边过，
水调声长醉里听。
款举金觥劝，
谁是当筵最有情？

李璟

应天长

一钩初月临妆镜，
蝉鬓凤钗慵不整。
重帘静，层楼迥，
惆怅落花风不定。

柳堤芳草径，
梦断辘轳金井。
昨夜更阑酒醒，
春愁过却病。

望远行

玉砌花光锦绣明，
朱扉长日镇长扃。
夜寒不去寝难成，
炉香烟冷自亭亭。

残月秣陵砧，
不传消息但传情。
黄金窗下忽然惊，
征人归日二毛生。

浣溪沙

手卷真珠上玉钩，
依前春恨锁重楼。
风里落花谁是主？
思悠悠！

青鸟不传云外信，
丁香空结雨中愁。
回首绿波三楚暮，
接天流。

浣溪沙

菡萏香销翠叶残，
西风愁起绿波间。
还与韶光共憔悴，
不堪看。

细雨梦回鸡塞远，
小楼吹彻玉笙寒。
多少泪珠何限恨！
倚阑干。

浣溪沙

红日已高三丈透，
金炉次第添香兽，
红锦地衣随步皱。

佳人舞点金钗溜，
酒恶时拈花蕊嗅，
别殿遥闻箫鼓奏。

一斛珠

晚妆初过，
沉檀轻注些儿个。
向人微露丁香颗，
一曲清歌，
暂引樱桃破。

罗袖裛残殷色可，
杯深旋被香醪涴。
绣床斜凭娇无那，
烂嚼红茸，
笑向檀郎唾。

玉楼春

晚妆初了明肌雪，
春殿嫔娥鱼贯列。
凤箫吹断水云间，
重按霓裳歌遍彻。

临春谁更飘香屑？
醉拍栏杆情味切。
归时休放烛花红，
待踏马蹄清夜月。

菩萨蛮

寻春须是先春早，
看花莫待花枝老。
缥色玉柔擎，
醅浮盏面清。

何妨频笑粲？
禁苑春归晚。
同醉与闲平，
诗随羯鼓成。

菩萨蛮

花明月暗笼轻雾，
今宵好向郎边去。
刬袜步香阶，
手提金缕鞋。

画堂南畔见，
一向偎人颤。
奴为出来难，
教君恣意怜。

菩萨蛮

蓬莱院闭天台女，
画堂昼寝人无语。
抛枕翠云光，
绣衣闻异香。

潜来珠锁动，
惊觉银屏梦。
脸慢笑盈盈，
相看无限情。

菩萨蛮

铜簧韵脆锵寒竹，
新声慢奏移纤玉。
眼色暗相钩，
秋波横欲流。

雨云深绣户，
来便谐衷素。
宴罢又成空，
魂迷春梦中。

喜迁莺

晓月坠，宿云微，
无语枕频欹。
梦回芳草思依依，
天远雁声稀。

啼莺散，余花乱，
寂寞画堂深院。
片红休扫尽从伊，
留待舞人归。

采桑子

亭前春逐红英尽，
舞态徘徊。
细雨霏微，
不放双眉时暂开。

绿窗冷静芳音断，
香印成灰。
可奈情怀？
欲睡朦胧入梦来。

长相思

云一绹，玉一梭。
淡淡衫儿薄薄罗。
轻颦双黛螺。

秋风多，雨相和。
帘外芭蕉三两窠。
夜长人奈何！

渔父

浪花有意千重雪，
桃李无言一队春。
一壶酒，一竿纶，
快活如侬有几人？

渔父

一棹春风一叶舟，
一纶茧缕一轻钩。
花满渚，酒满瓯，
万顷波中得自由。

谢新恩

秦楼不见吹箫女，
空余上苑风光。
粉英金蕊自低昂。
东风恼我，
才发一衿香。

琼窗梦笛残日，
当年得恨何长！
碧栏杆外映垂杨。
暂时相见，
如梦懒思量。

谢新恩

樱花落尽阶前月，
象床愁倚薰笼。
远似去年今日恨还同。

双鬟不整云憔悴，
泪沾红抹胸。
何处相思苦？
纱窗醉梦中。

谢新恩

庭空客散人归后，
画堂半掩珠帘。
林风淅淅夜厌厌。
小楼新月，
回首自纤纤。

春光镇在人空老，
新愁往恨何穷！
金窗力困起还慵。
一声羌笛，
惊起醉怡容。

谢新恩

樱花落尽春将困，
秋千架下归时。
漏暗斜月迟迟花在枝。

……
彻晓纱窗下，
待来君不知。

谢新恩

冉冉秋光留不住，
满阶红叶暮。
又是过重阳，
台榭登临处。

茱萸香坠，
紫菊气，飘庭户，
晚烟笼细雨。
雍雍新雁咽寒声，
愁恨年年长相似。

阮郎归

东风吹水日衔山，
春来长是闲。
落花狼藉酒阑珊，
笙歌醉梦间。

佩声悄，晚妆残，
凭谁整翠鬟？
留连光景惜朱颜，
黄昏独倚阑。

蝶恋花

遥夜亭皋闲信步。
乍过清明,
渐觉伤春暮。
数点雨声风约住,
朦胧淡月云来去。

桃李依依春暗度。
谁上秋千,
笑里低低语?
一寸芳心千万缕,
人间没个安排处。

捣练子

深院静，小庭空，
断续寒砧断续风。
无奈夜长人不寐，
数声和月到帘栊。

捣练子

云鬓乱，晚妆残，
带恨眉儿远岫攒。
斜托香腮春笋嫩，
为谁和泪倚栏杆？

清平乐

别来春半，触目愁肠断。
砌下落梅如雪乱，
拂了一身还满。

雁来音信无凭，
路遥归梦难成。
离恨恰如春草，
更行更远还生。

采桑子

辘轳金井梧桐晚，
几树惊秋。
昼雨新愁，
百尺虾须在玉钩。

琼窗春断双蛾皱，
回首边头。
欲寄鳞游，
九曲寒波不泝流。

临江仙

樱桃落尽春归去，
蝶翻金粉双飞。
子规啼月小楼西。
画帘珠箔，
惆怅暮烟垂。

门巷寂寥人散后，
望残烟草低迷。
何时重听玉骢嘶？
扑帘飞絮，
依约梦回时！

乌夜啼

昨夜风兼雨，
帘帏飒飒秋声。
烛残漏断频欹枕，
起坐不能平。

世事漫随流水，
算来梦里浮生。
醉乡路稳宜频到，
此外不堪行。

虞美人

风回小院庭芜绿，
柳眼春相续。
凭栏半日独无言，
依旧竹声新月似当年。

笙歌未散尊罍在，
池面冰初解。
烛明香暗画楼深，
满鬓清霜残雪思难任。

破阵子

四十年来家国，
三千里地山河。
凤阁龙楼连霄汉，
玉树琼枝作烟萝。
几曾识干戈？

一旦归为臣虏，
沈腰潘鬓消磨。
最是仓皇辞庙日，
教坊犹奏别离歌。
垂泪对宫娥。

望江南

闲梦远，
南国正芳春。
船上管弦江面绿，
满城飞絮滚轻尘。
忙杀看花人。

望江南

闲梦远，
南国正清秋。
千里江山寒色远，
芦花深处泊孤舟。
笛在月明楼。

梦江南

多少恨，
昨夜梦魂中。
还似旧时游上苑，
车如流水马如龙，
花月正春风。

梦江南

多少泪，
断脸复横颐。
心事莫将和泪说，
凤笙休向泪时吹，
肠断更无疑。

乌夜啼

林花谢了春红，
太匆匆。
无奈朝来寒雨晚来风。

胭脂泪，留人醉，
几时重？
自是人生长恨水长东。

乌夜啼

无言独上西楼，
月如钩。
寂寞梧桐深院锁清秋。

剪不断，理还乱，
是离愁，
别是一般滋味在心头。

子夜歌

人生愁恨何能免？
销魂独我情何限！
故国梦重归，
觉来双泪垂！

高楼谁与上？
长记秋晴望。
往事已成空，
还如一梦中！

浪淘沙

往事只堪哀，
对景难排。
秋风庭院藓侵阶。
一任珠帘闲不卷，
终日谁来？

金锁已沉埋，
壮气蒿莱。
晚凉天静月华开。
想得玉楼瑶殿影，
空照秦淮。

虞美人

春花秋月何时了？
往事知多少！
小楼昨夜又东风，
故国不堪回首月明中。

雕栏玉砌应犹在，
只是朱颜改。
问君能有几多愁？
恰似一江春水向东流。

浪淘沙

帘外雨潺潺，
春意阑珊，
罗衾不耐五更寒。
梦里不知身是客，
一晌贪欢。

独自莫凭栏，
无限江山，
别时容易见时难。
流水落花春去也，
天上人间！

无名氏

后庭宴

千里故乡，
十年华屋，
乱魂飞过屏山簇。
眼重眉褪不胜春，
菱花知我销香玉。

双双燕子归来，
应解笑人幽独。
断歌零舞，
遗恨清江曲。
万树绿低迷，
一庭红扑簌。

THEORY ON LITERARY TRANSLATION OF THE CHINESE SCHOOL

The theory on literary translation of the Chinese school owes its origin to traditional Chinese culture, including the Confucian and the Taoist school of thought respectively represented by *Thus Spoke the Master* and *Laws Divine and Human*.

It is said in the first chapter of *Laws Divine and Human* that truth can be known, but it may not be the truth you know, and that things may be named, but names are not the things. When applied to literary translation, this may mean that the theory on literary translation can be known, but it may not the unproven theory on the one hand, nor the scientific theory on the other, for neither literary translation nor its theory is science. As the names are not equal to the things, the translation cannot be equal to the original. As there is more difference than equivalence between the Chinese and the English language, the principle of equivalence can not be applied to the translation between them as between two occidental languages.

It is said in the last chapter of *Laws Divine and Human* that truthful words may not be beautiful and beautiful words may not be truthful. That is to say, there is contradiction between truth and beauty or between equivalence and excellence. A translation where equivalents are used may be called a faithful or truthful translation. When no equivalent can be found between two languages, the translator should make use of the best expressions or excellent expressions of the target language. That may be called theory of excellence.

In *Thus Spoke the Master*, Confucius said, "At seventy, I can do what I will without going beyond what is right." Professor Zhu Guangqian said that this has shown the mature state of an artist. I think it may also show the mature state of a literary translator. The literal translator has used the equivalents without going beyond the original in sound; the liberal translator has described the image without going beyond the original in sense; the literary translator has described the scene without going beyond reality. Not to go beyond the original is to be truthful or faithful, and the translator has reached the ordinary level of translation. To do what one will without going beyond the original is not only to be faithful but also to make his translation beautiful, in that case the translator has attained a higher level. To excel the original without going beyond the reality it describes is to attain the highest level.

What is literary translation? It is an art of solving the contradiction between faithfulness (or truth) and beauty. How to solve it? There are three methods, namely, equalization, generalization and particularization. When there is little or no contradition between truth and beauty, equalization or equivalents may be used. When there is contradction between them, generalization may be used to make the meaning clear, and particularization to make a deeper impression.

Confucius said in *Thus Spoke the Master* that it would be good to be understandable, better to be enjoyable and best to be delectable or delightful. When applied to literary translation, this principle means that an understandable translation is good, an enjoyable one is better and a delightful one is best. The ontology or theory of contradition between truth and beauty, the methodology or theory of equalization, generalization and particularization, and the teleology or theory of the understandable, the enjoyable and the delectable, all owe their origin to the Confucian and Taoist schools of thoughts.

But Confucius said less about what delight is and more about how to be delightful. In the beginning of *Thus Spoke the Master* he said it is delightful to acquire knowledge and put it into practice; In Chapter Six he told us how Yan Hui could find delight in reading though living in a humble lane with only a handful of rice to eat and a gourdful of water to drink; In Chapter Eleven, Zeng Xi told us his delight in an spring excursion. From these examples we can see Confucius' theory on delight or teleology, and his theory on practice or methodology. His theory is not scientific but artistic. Since literary translation is an art but not a branch of science, his theory can not only be applied to the practice but also to the theory of literary translation. As his theory has stood the test of time, it is as durable as scientific theories. A theorist on science who studies truth and the truthful should not go beyond what is truthful. A theorist on art or an artist who studies beauty and the beautiful may go beyond what is truthful and faithful.

The contradiction between truth and beauty in Chinese theory on literary translation has developed into a contradiction between equivalence and excellence. As Keats said, "Beauty is truth, truth beauty," we may even say beauty is a virtue, a kind of excellence. When we cannot find the equivalent, we may resort to generalization or particularization.

In short, literary translation is an art to create the beautiful. This is the epistemology of the Chinese school. The contradition between truth and beauty or between equivalence and excellence is its ontology; the theory on equalization, generalization and particularization is its triple methodology; and the theory of the understandable, the enjoyable and the delectable or delightful is its triple teleology.

Xu Yuanchong
Oct. 2011

代后记：中国学派的文学翻译理论

中国学派的文学翻译理论源自中国的传统文化，主要包括儒家思想和道家思想，儒家思想的代表著作是《论语》，道家思想的代表著作是《老子道德经》。

《老子道德经》第一章开始就说："道可道，非常道；名可名，非常名。"联系到翻译理论上来，就是说：翻译理论是可以知道的，是可以说得出来的，但不是只说得出来而经不起实践检验的空头理论，这就是中国学派翻译理论中的实践论。其次，文学翻译理论不能算科学理论（自然科学），与其说是社会科学理论，不如说是人文学科或艺术理论，这就是文学翻译的艺术论，也可以说是相对论。后六个字"名可名，非常名"应用到文学翻译理论上来，可以有两层意思：第一层是原文的文字是描写现实的，但并不等于现实，文字和现实之间还有距离，还有矛盾；第二层意思是译文和原文之间也有距离，也有矛盾，译文和原文所描写的现实之间，自然还有距离，还有矛盾。译文应该发挥译语优势，运用最好的译语表达方式，来和原文展开竞赛，使译文和现实的距离或矛盾小于原文和现实之间的矛盾，那就是超越原文了。这就是文学翻译理论中的优势论或优化论，超越论或竞赛论。文学翻译理论应该解决的不只是译文和原文在文字方面的矛盾，还要解决译文和原文所反映的现实之间的矛盾，这是文学翻译的本体论。

一般翻译只要解决"真"或"信"或"似"的问题，文学翻译却要解决"真"或"信"和"美"之间的矛盾。原文反映的现实不只是言内之意，还有言外之意。中国的文学语言往往有言外之意，甚至还有言外之情。文学翻译理论也要解决译文和原文的言外之意、言外之情的矛盾。

《论语》说："知之者不如好之者，好之者不如乐之者。"知之，好之，乐之，这"三之论"是对艺术论的进一步说明。艺术论第一条原则要求译文忠实于原文所反映的现实，求的是真，可以使人知之；第二条原则要求用"三化"法来优化译文，求的是美，可以使人好之；第三条原则要求用"三美"来优化译文，尤其是译诗词，求的是意美、音美和形美，可以使人乐之。如果"不逾矩"的等化译文能使人知之（理解），那就达到了文学翻译的低标准，如从心所欲而不逾矩的浅化或深化的译文既能使人知之，又能使人好之（喜欢），那就达到了中标准；如果从心所欲的译文不但能使人知之，好之，还能使人乐之（愉快），那才达到了文学翻译的高标准。这也是中国译者对世界译论作出的贡献。

翻译艺术的规律是从心所欲而不逾矩。"矩"就是规矩，规律。但艺术规律却可以依人的主观意志而转移，是因为得到承认才算正确的。所以贝多芬说：为了更美，没有什么清规戒律不可打破。他所说的戒律不是科学规律，而是艺术规律。不能用科学规律来评论文学翻译。

孔子不大谈"什么是"（What?）而多谈"怎么做"（How?）。这是中国传统的方法论，比西方流传更久，影响更广，作用更大，并且经过了两三千年实践的考验。《论语》第一章中说："学而时习之，不亦说（悦，乐）乎！""学"是取得知识，"习"是实践。孔子只说学习实践可以得到乐趣，却不说什么是"乐"。这就是孔子的方法论，是中国文学翻译理论的依据。

总而言之，中国学派的文学翻译理论是研究老子提出的

"信"（似）"美"（优）矛盾的艺术（本体论），但"信"不限原文，还指原文所反映的现实，这是认识论，"信"由严复提出的"信达雅"发展到鲁迅提出"信顺"的直译，再发展到陈源的"三似"（形似，意似，神似），直到傅雷的"重神似不重形似"，这已经接近"美"了。"美"发展到鲁迅的"三美"（意美，音美，形美），再发展到林语堂提出的"忠实，通顺，美"，转化为朱生豪"传达原作意趣"的意译，直到茅盾提出的"美的享受"。孔子提出的"从心所欲"发展到郭沫若提出的创译论（好的翻译等于创作），以及钱钟书说的译文可以胜过原作的"化境"说，再发展到优化论，超越论，"三化"（等化，浅化，深化）方法论。孔子提出的"不逾矩"和老子说的"信言不美，美言不信"有同有异。老子"信美"并重，孔子"从心所欲"重于"不逾矩"，发展为朱光潜的"艺术论"，包括郭沫若说的"在信达之外，愈雅愈好。所谓'雅'不是高深或讲修饰，而是文学价值或艺术价值比较高。"直到茅盾说的："必须把文学翻译工作提高到艺术创造的水平。"孔子的"乐之"发展为胡适之的"愉快"说（翻译要使读者读得愉快），再发展到"三之"（知之，好之，乐之）目的论。这就是中国学派的文学翻译理论发展为"美化之艺术"（"三美"，"三化"，"三之"的艺术）的概况。

许渊冲
2011年10月

图书在版编目（CIP）数据

唐五代词选: 汉英对照 / 许渊冲译. —2版. —北京: 五洲传播出版社, 2019.6
ISBN 978-7-5085-4207-2

Ⅰ.①唐… Ⅱ.①许… Ⅲ.①五代词－选集－汉、英
Ⅳ.①I222.843.1

中国版本图书馆CIP数据核字(2019)第098672号

唐五代词选

译　　者：许渊冲
策划编辑：荆孝敏　郑　磊
责任编辑：王　峰
中文编辑：张敏杰
英文编辑：马培武　鲁大东
装帧设计：北京正视文化艺术有限责任公司
出版发行：五洲传播出版社
地　　址：北京市海淀区北三环中路31号生产力大楼B座6层
邮　　编：100088
电　　话：010-82005927，010-82007837
网　　址：http://www.cicc.org.cn http://www.thatsbooks.com
印　　刷：中煤（北京）印务有限公司
版　　次：2012年1月第1版 2019年6月第2版第1次印刷
开　　本：140mm×210mm 1/32
印　　张：6.5
字　　数：170千字
书　　号：ISBN 978-7-5085-4207-2
定　　价：79.00元